For Carl, who believes in me
—B.C.S.

To Zoey, Chase, and Brooke, the center of my universe
—M.R.

Text copyright © 2020 by Brianna Caplan Sayres
Jacket art and interior illustrations copyright © 2020 by Merrill Rainey

Intergalactic Afikoman
1037 NE 65th Street, #167
Seattle, WA 98115

www.IntergalacticAfikoman.com

Designed by Whitney Manger

Publisher's Cataloging-In-Publication Data

Names: Sayres, Brianna Caplan, author. | Rainey, Merrill, illustrator.
Title: Asteroid Goldberg : Passover in outer space / by Brianna Caplan
    Sayres ; illustrated by Merrill Rainey.
Description: First edition. | Seattle : Intergalactic Afikoman, [2020] |
    Interest age level: 004-008.
Identifiers: ISBN 9781951365004 | ISBN 9781951365011 (ebook)
Subjects: LCSH: Passover—Juvenile fiction. | Passover food—Juvenile
    fiction. | Jewish families—Juvenile fiction. | Outer space—
    Juvenile fiction. | CYAC: Passover—Fiction. | Passover food—Fiction. | Jewish
    families—Fiction. | Outer space—Fiction. | LCGFT: Stories in rhyme. |
    Fantasy fiction.
Classification: LCC PZ8.3.S274 As 2020 (print) | LCC PZ8.3.S274 (ebook) |
    DDC [E]—dc23

Library of Congress Control Number: 2019915617
Printed in the USA
2 4 6 8 10 9 7 5 3 1
First Edition

# ASTEROID
## GOLDBERG
### Passover in Outer Space

by Brianna Caplan Sayres

illustrated by Merrill Rainey

INTERGALACTIC Afikoman

SEATTLE

EARTH
4.67 BILLION MILES

Asteroid and her parents
enjoyed their galactic flight,
as she zipped them home from Pluto
to prepare for seder night.

Oy! Passover in outer space
was not what they had planned!

What would a seder be in space?
The grown-ups had no clue.
But their space-whiz, Asteroid,
took a more creative view.

She flung the fridge door open.
Pastrami flew from rye.
Bagels floated far from lox. . .

She watched their chametz fly!
"Where will we find Pesach food?"
asked her parents with dismay.

She aimed their ship toward Jupiter.
So many yummy moons!

"Matzoh balls!" said Asteroid.
"All we need are spoons!"

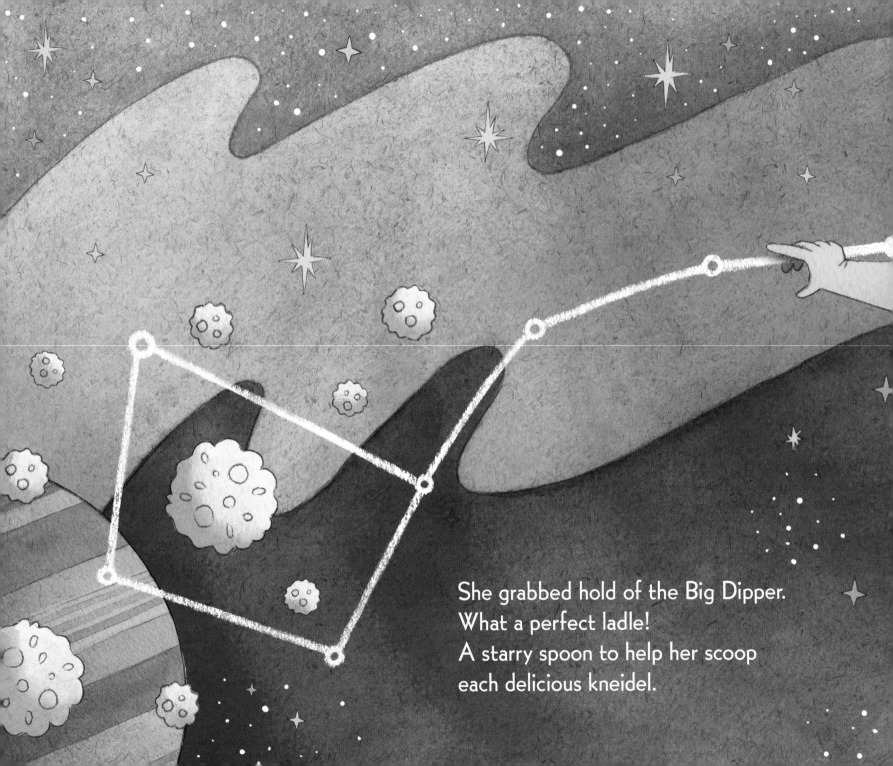

She grabbed hold of the Big Dipper.
What a perfect ladle!
A starry spoon to help her scoop
each delicious kneidel.

Now where could she find matzoh?
She couldn't wait to munch.
She broke a piece off Saturn's rings—
The perfect Pesach crunch!

Then she headed back to Jupiter
with its spot, horseradish red.
Such a tasty bitter herb
for their unleavened bread!

Now their food was almost ready.
It would soon be seder night.

She peered into her telescope.
What guests could she invite?

Grandma Luna
biked on Venus.

Uncle Cosmos
hiked on Mars.

Aunt Andromeda and
Cousin Corona were giving
tours of all the stars.

Each guest opened a haggadah,
sang the order of the evening,
then drank from a space-kiddush cup
while zero-gravity leaning.

Soon Dad hid the afikoman
and reminded them, "No peeking."
This would be Asteroid's first seder
with intergalactic seeking!

Mah Nishtanah came next.
Asteroid started to sing.

What makes this night so different?

The answer:

Everything!

Asteroid acted out the story
of Egyptian slavery.
Without the pull of gravity,
she really did feel free.

Finally came dinner,
which was just a bit bizarre.
She liked her matzoh balls to float,
but this might go too far!

Asteroid popped the hatch for Elijah's space debut. She looked outside and heard a voice. . .

It was Houston coming through.

The Goldberg ship can land.

But Asteroid shouted

NO!

This seder wasn't long enough!
It can't be time to go!"

Asteroid said, "Let's stay the week,
then head on back to base."
And her family all agreed,

NEXT YEAR IN OUTER

SPACE!

## How is this seder different from every other seder?

It's in space, of course! And Jupiter's moons are the matzoh balls! But a seder can be creative no matter what planet it is on. For more creative seder ideas, and for some out-of-this-world (and completely true) information about Jewish traditions and Jewish astronauts in space, please check out www.IntergalacticAfikoman.com.

## GLOSSARY

**afikoman**—the broken piece of matzoh eaten at the end of the seder

**chametz**—leavened food, not eaten during Passover

**haggadah**—the book read during the seder

**kiddush**—the blessing over the wine or grape juice

**kneidel**—the Yiddish word for a matzoh ball

**Mah Nishtanah**—often referred to as the four questions, traditionally asked by the youngest person at the seder

**matzoh**—unleavened bread

**oy**—a Yiddish exclamation, indicates distress

**Pesach**—the Hebrew word for Passover

**seder**—means "order"; the special meal and rituals done on Passover night

**BRIANNA CAPLAN SAYRES** would love to spend Passover in outer space, but for now, she enjoys celebrating seder with her husband and their two future astronauts in her hometown, Seattle, Washington. Brianna is the author of picture books including the *Where Do Diggers Sleep at Night?* series illustrated by Christian Slade and *Night Night, Curiosity* illustrated by Ryan O'Rourke. You can visit Brianna at her playground on the web, www.briannacaplansayres.com.

Growing up, **MERRILL RAINEY** spent most of his Saturday afternoons watching monster movies, drawing superheroes, and going on imaginary adventures with his siblings. Today, he is a cowboy-boot-wearing, award-winning illustrator, designer, and paper engineer. Merrill likes to experiment with art tools and uses marker, cut paper, and water soluble graphite to create his illustrations. Merrill is the creator of Color-Cut-Create! a Paper Toy Activity Book. He lives in the historic town of Maumee, Ohio with his editor (his wife), subject matter experts (his kids), and very opinionated coworkers (two pups, two goldfish, and some crabby hermit crabs).